Mr. Snow Bunting's SECRET

story and pictures by

ROBERT QUACKENBUSH

Lothrop, Lee & Shepard Company
A Division of William Morrow & Company, Inc.
NEW YORK

Other Fun-to-Read Books by Robert Quackenbush

ANIMAL CRACKS
DETECTIVE MOLE
DETECTIVE MOLE
And The Secret Clues
PETE PACK RAT
PETE PACK RAT
And The Gila Monster Gang
SHERIFF SALLY GOPHER
And The Haunted Dance Hall

Library of Congress Cataloging in Publication Data
Quackenbush, Robert M.
Mr. Snow Bunting's secret.
(A Fun-to-read book)
SUMMARY: The mysterious Mr. Snow Bunting's secret method for wrapping gifts charms the town and arouses the jealous suspicions of Mr. Dog.
[1. Gift wrappings—Fiction. 2. Christmas stories. 3. Animals—Fiction] I. Title.
PZ7.Q16Mi [E] 77-15951
ISBN 0-688-41835-X
ISBN 0-688-51835-4 lib. bdg.

Printed in the United States of America.

First Edition
1 2 3 4 5 6 7 8 9 10

CONTENTS

POST OF
MR. SNOW BUNTIN
GIFTWRAPPING
Open

1

THE NEW SHOP IN TOWN

When the last of the winter snow melted, Mr. Snow Bunting came to town and opened a shop. The sign in his window said:

MR. SNOW BUNTING
GIFT WRAPPING
FOR ALL OCCASIONS
Open March to November

Mrs. Hen was the first to notice the new shop.

"My goodness," Mrs. Hen said as
she looked at Mr. Snow Bunting's
window display. "What beautiful
packages! Such lovely bows!"
Just then Mr. Dog and Mr. Cat
came out of the post office
next door to the shop.
Mr. Cat was carrying an armload
of Easter cards and packages,
but Mr. Dog had none.
Mr. Dog never got any mail.
That was because he never wrote
anyone or gave anyone presents.
But Mr. Dog thought it was the
fault of the post office.

He had just been there to complain about it again to Postmistress Pigeon.
"Mr. Dog! Mr. Cat! Come this way," Mrs. Hen called. "I want to show you something."

Mr. Dog and Mr. Cat came over
to Mr. Snow Bunting's shop
and looked in the window.
"Isn't this terrific?" said
Mrs. Hen. "There isn't anyone in
town who can tie a bow, much less
big, fluffy bows like these."
"Humph!" said Mr. Dog. "What's
so great about that? I bet I
could tie a bow like those if
I wanted to. But why would I
want to?"

Mrs. Hen and Mr. Cat paid no
attention.
They were used to Mr. Dog.

"I think I'll go in," said
Mrs. Hen. "I have some Easter
gifts here for the chicks."
Mr. Cat went inside with her.
Mr. Dog stayed outside.
"How do you do," said Mrs. Hen
to Mr. Snow Bunting.
"Pleased to meet you," Mr. Snow
Bunting said. "May I help you?"

Mrs. Hen reached into her
shopping bag and took out the
chicks' presents.
"Let me be your first customer,"
she said. "Please gift wrap
these for me."
"With pleasure," said Mr. Snow
Bunting. "What cute Easter hats."
Mr. Snow Bunting put each hat
in a box and wrapped them all.
Then he took the packages behind
a curtain at the back of the shop.
When he brought them out, each
box was tied with a fancy bow.
"How pretty," said Mrs. Hen.
"How much do I owe you?"

"Twenty-five cents each, please,"
said Mr. Snow Bunting.
"That's a fair price," said Mrs.
Hen, reaching into her purse.
"Your shop should do well.
But does your sign mean you will
be here only until November?"

"Yes," said Mr. Snow Bunting. "My winter home is up North. I must go there when the first snow of winter comes. Next spring I will visit another town."

"Well, we are glad to have you here for as long as you can stay," said Mrs. Hen.

"If you don't mind my asking," said Mr. Cat politely, "just how do you make those bows?"

"I don't mind your asking," Mr. Snow Bunting said, "but I'm afraid I can't tell you. That's my secret!"

MR. SNOW BUNTING
Gift Wrapping for all occasions
open March to November
(approximately)

2

THE JEALOUS BYSTANDER

When Mrs. Hen and Mr. Cat came out of the shop, Mr. Dog was waiting for them.

"Well," he said, "did you find out how Mr. Snow Bunting makes bows? And why his shop closes for the Christmas season, just at the busiest time?"

Mr. Cat told Mr. Dog what Mr. Snow Bunting had said.

“Hmmm,” said Mr. Dog. “That sounds pretty fishy to me. Who ever heard of a bird going north for the winter? And what is so secret about making a bow?”

Mr. Cat and Mrs. Hen made no reply, and went on their way.

Mr. Dog hung around Mr. Snow Bunting’s shop all day.

Customers streamed in and out. Mrs. Hen and Mr. Cat had told everyone about the shop.

By late afternoon, a long line of
customers was waiting to get in.
"I wish I had a shop with
customers making such a big fuss
over *me*," Mr. Dog said to himself.
Then he saw Mrs. Goose
coming out of the shop.
She was covered with bows!

"Oh, no!" said Mr. Dog. "In one day, bows have taken over the town. Next, they'll rename it Bowtown. I *must* figure out how to tie bows like Mr. Snow Bunting."

Mr. Dog went to the dime store and came back with a spool of ribbon. He sat on the curb and set to work.

"What is Mr. Dog doing?" Mr. Elephant asked Mr. Peacock, who was standing next to him in line.

"I think he is trying to tie a bow," said Mr. Peacock. "But he doesn't seem to be having much luck."

MR·SNO

Mr. Dog struggled and struggled.
It grew dark, and the shops and
stores were closing.
Even Mr. Snow Bunting
closed up for the night.
He went to his room
above his shop.
Soon everyone had gone home.

By this time, Mr. Dog was hot
and cross.
The ribbon was twisted around
his head, his waist, and his tail.
Still Mr. Dog would not give up.
Finally, he got so tangled up he
couldn't move.
Who would untie him?

At last, Postmistress Pigeon
came by after locking up for
the night.
"Good golly, Mr. Dog," she said.
"What are you doing all tied up
like that? Do you want me to
mail you somewhere?"
"Just kindly untie me!" barked
Mr. Dog.

3

THE GUST OF WIND

When summer came, Mr. Snow
Bunting was as busy as before.
There were presents to be wrapped
for birthdays, weddings, and
graduations.
On the Fourth of July, Mr. Snow
Bunting was asked to make bows
to decorate the bandstand
for the town's annual picnic.
Mr. Dog was more jealous than ever.

Then one day in August, Mr. Dog
met Mr. Cat in the post office.
Mr. Cat invited Mr. Dog to a
surprise birthday party he and
Mrs. Cat were giving for Mrs. Hen.
"Please bring a present, Mr. Dog,"
said Mr. Cat. "Mr. Snow Bunting
will gift wrap it free of charge.
That's because Mrs. Hen was his
very first customer."
"I'll have to think about it,"
snapped Mr. Dog.
On the day of the party,
Mr. Dog gave in.

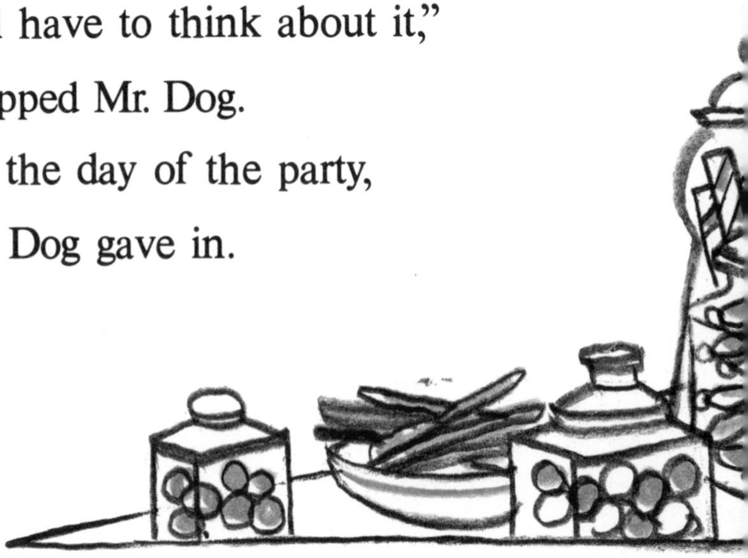

He went to Mr. Toad's candy
store and bought a bag of
corn candy for Mrs. Hen.
It was her favorite kind.
"Don't you have anything besides
a paper bag, Mr. Toad?" asked
Mr. Dog.
"Let Mr. Snow Bunting gift wrap
it for you," said Mr. Toad.

There was nothing else to do!
Mr. Dog took the candy to Mr. Snow Bunting's shop.
He gritted his teeth and went inside.

"I want this put in a box and
a-a-a bow on top," Mr. Dog
blurted out. "It's for Mrs. Hen."
"Gladly," said Mr. Snow Bunting.
He poured the candy into a box
covered with foil.
Just as Mr. Snow Bunting was
about to take the box behind the
curtain for a bow, he glanced
out the front window.
"Oh, excuse me for a moment," he
said to Mr. Dog. "There goes Mr.
Elephant. I must give him a book
he left here this morning."
Mr. Snow Bunting ran out of the
shop, leaving the door wide open.

Suddenly, a gust of wind blew in.
The wind lifted the curtain that
hid the place where Mr. Snow
Bunting tied his bows.

Mr. Dog saw everything!
He saw a worktable and spools
of ribbon.
He saw a pair of scissors.
Then Mr. Dog gasped.
He saw a red, pointed cap!
There was something else on
the worktable, too.
But before he could see what
it was, the curtain blew down.
At that moment, Mr. Snow Bunting
came back in and shut the door.
"Thank you for waiting, Mr. Dog,"
he said. "I'll have Mrs. Hen's gift
ready for you in a jiffy."

4

THE LUCKY BREAK

At Mrs. Hen's party, Mr. Dog
was bursting to tell what
he had seen behind the curtain
in Mr. Snow Bunting's shop.
The red, pointed cap could
mean only one thing.
Mr. Snow Bunting was a sorcerer!
He made the bows by using magic!
He had put a spell on the town,
to make everyone come to his shop.

"But I need more proof before I
can say anything," Mr. Dog
thought. "A closer look at that
worktable should turn up something.
Then the town will make me a hero
for exposing a dangerous sorcerer!"
Mr. Dog tried to think of a way
to get the proof he needed.
He could think of nothing else.
Days and weeks passed, but he
still had not found a way.
Then early one morning just
before Halloween, Mr. Dog saw a
note on the public notice board
in the post office.

The note said:

HELP NEEDED WITH PACKING
FOR ONE EVENING. THE PAY
IS FIVE DOLLARS.
SEE MR. SNOW BUNTING

"This is my break," said Mr. Dog.

When Postmistress Pigeon wasn't
looking, Mr. Dog grabbed the
note and hid it in his paw
before anyone else saw it.
In a flash, Mr. Dog ran out of the
post office and down the street
to Mr. Horse's costume shop.
He bought a rabbit costume
and then went home to wait
until it got dark.
At nightfall, Mr. Dog put on his
costume and headed for Mr. Snow
Bunting's shop.
He dodged among the shadows
to keep from being seen.

When he reached the shop, he
knocked on the door.
Mr. Snow Bunting answered it.

Mr. Dog disguised his voice.
"I saw your note in the post office," he said. "I would like the job."
"Wonderful," said Mr. Snow Bunting. "Step right in."
Mr. Dog followed Mr. Snow Bunting to the back of the shop.
"I need these gift boxes and spools of ribbon packed for mailing," Mr. Snow Bunting said. "I'll be leaving soon, and I want them to get to my home up North before I do."
Mr. Dog's heart pounded.

He was going to be working where
he could get a clear view of the
worktable behind the curtain!

For several hours, Mr. Dog
helped Mr. Snow Bunting pack.
Every chance he got, Mr. Dog
would glance at the worktable.
He saw the red cap, and something
else that made him shiver.
It was a cardboard cutout in the
shape of Mr. Snow Bunting himself!

Mr. Dog hurried to finish the packing.
Mr. Snow Bunting walked him to the door and paid him.
"Thank you for helping me," Mr. Snow Bunting said. "By the way, Mr. Dog, I like your costume. Are you wearing it on Halloween?"
Mr. Dog nearly fell over.
Without saying a word, he ran down the street as fast as he could.
"I was right," thought Mr. Dog. "Mr. Snow Bunting is a sorcerer. That cardboard cutout proves it. And how else could he have seen through my disguise?"

CES
STAMPS & PARCEL POST

5

THE WARNING POSTER

The next day, Mr. Dog hurried up the street to the post office. He pushed his way through the crowd to the window marked

STAMPS AND PARCEL POST.

"I want to put this on the public notice board," Mr. Dog said to Postmistress Pigeon. He held up a poster.

Everyone in the post office
gathered around to read the poster.
In big red letters it said:

PARENTS! DO NOT LET YOUR
CHILDREN GO TRICK-OR-TREATING
TONIGHT AT MR. SNOW BUNTING'S
SHOP. HE IS A SORCERER!

"You can't put up a poster like
that, Mr. Dog!" everyone cried.
Postmistress Pigeon was
flabbergasted.
"Have you gone crazy, Mr. Dog?"
she said. "How can you even
think such an awful thing about
Mr. Snow Bunting?"
Mr. Dog sputtered.
"I know what I saw," he said,
"and I saw proof that Mr. Snow
Bunting is a sorcerer! He has
the whole town under a spell!
Behind that curtain in his shop
he keeps a strange cardboard
bird and a red, pointed cap!"

"Like the cap I have on, Mr. Dog?"
said a familiar voice.
Mr. Dog whirled around.

Mr. Snow Bunting and Mr. Elephant
had just come in the door.
Mr. Elephant was carrying the
boxes Mr. Dog had helped to pack.
Mr. Snow Bunting touched his cap.
"That's the first time anyone ever
called my cap a sorcerer's hat,"
he said. "Today I'm wearing it
to keep my head warm. But I can
see Mr. Dog will be very unhappy
unless he knows just why I happen
to have a cap like this."
Mr. Snow Bunting took Mr. Dog
aside and whispered something.
Mr. Dog's jaw dropped.

"And that is why I have this cap," Mr. Snow Bunting finished. He stepped up to the window to mail his packages. When Postmistress Pigeon read the address on the labels, her jaw dropped, too.

She gave Mr. Dog a quick look.
They both knew something about
Mr. Snow Bunting that no one
else knew.
Postmistress Pigeon put stamps
on the packages.
Mr. Snow Bunting paid her,
nodded to everyone, and went out.
"Good heavens, Mr. Dog," said
Mrs. Hen. "What did Mr. Snow
Bunting tell you to make you
look so pale?"
"I can't tell you," said Mr.
Dog. "I can only say I am
very sorry that I ever thought
unkindly of Mr. Snow Bunting."

TRICK OR TREAT

6

THE SURPRISE PRESENT

On Halloween night, everyone
went trick-or-treating at
Mr. Snow Bunting's shop.
Mr. Snow Bunting was ready.
He gave out candy tied with bows.
"Will you really be leaving us
soon?" everyone asked him.
"I'm afraid so," said Mr. Snow
Bunting. "It's almost time for
the first snow of winter."

One night a couple of weeks later
it started to snow.
In the morning, Mr. Snow Bunting
was gone.

Mr. Dog and Postmistress Pigeon knew where Mr. Snow Bunting had gone, but they kept his secret. One thing still bothered Mr. Dog. Mr. Snow Bunting had explained the red, pointed cap. But what about the strange cardboard bird? That was still a mystery.

Thanksgiving came, and everyone began to get ready for Christmas. The holiday excitement helped everyone to forget how much they missed Mr. Snow Bunting.

Even Mr. Dog got into
the spirit of the season.
The day before Christmas, he
came into the post office
to mail some Christmas cards.
It was the first time he had
ever sent any!

"This card is for you, Ms. Pigeon,"
Mr. Dog said. "Have a Merry
Christmas."
"Same to you, Mr. Dog," said
Postmistress Pigeon. "And here
is a package for you. It just
came in today's mail."
"A package for *me*?" said Mr. Dog.
The package was marked:

DO NOT OPEN BEFORE CHRISTMAS.

Mr. Dog looked at the postmark.
Then he looked at Postmistress
Pigeon.
"Well," said Mr. Dog, "I guess
we both know who sent this."

That night Santa Claus came
riding through town.

The next morning, everyone got up early to see what Santa had put under the Christmas trees.

When they saw Santa's presents,
they all knew what Mr. Dog and
Postmistress Pigeon already knew.
All of Santa's presents were tied
with big fluffy bows.
Only Mr. Snow Bunting could
have tied them!
"Just think, Mama," cried Mrs.
Hen's chicks. "We have had one
of Santa's helpers right here
in this town!"
Mr. Dog was up early, too.
He could hardly wait to open his
package from the post office.
He tore off the outer wrapping.

Inside was a beautiful gift box.

It was tied with a big fluffy bow.

Mr. Dog lifted the lid.

Inside was the cardboard cutout

of Mr. Snow Bunting himself!

Attached was a note that said,

DEAR MR. DOG:

THANKS AGAIN FOR HELPING ME

PACK. THIS IS MY SECRET FOR

MAKING BOWS. NOW IT IS YOUR

SECRET, TOO. PLEASE TAKE OVER

FOR ME IN YOUR TOWN.

GOOD LUCK AND MERRY CHRISTMAS,

MR. SNOW BUNTING

To learn Mr. Snow Bunting's secret,
please turn the page.

INSTRUCTIONS

MR. SNOW BUNTING'S BOWMAKER

1. Cut a circle out of cardboard about as big as you want your bow to be. Cut a large "V" out of the circle. Then cut a notch on each side of the "V" so your bowmaker looks like the picture above.

2. To make a bow, insert one end of ribbon in notch and hold in place. Wind ribbon in and out in a figure 8 around the "wings."

3. When bow is full, snip the ribbon. Tie a small piece around the center of the bow (between the "wings") to hold it together.

4. Lift the bow off the bowmaker, fluff it, and tie or tape it to your package.

ROBERT QUACKENBUSH, author and illustrator of many Lothrop books, lives in New York City with his wife and son. About *Mr. Snow Bunting's Secret* he says, "I wanted to tell my son Piet about a secret of his great-grandmother's. Now it is your secret, too. But don't tell anyone!"

Other Fun-to-Read books by Mr. Quackenbush that you will enjoy are listed on the back of the title page.